Book One

into the garden

By Ashley-Lynn Hall

TRAVELING THE BIBLE

Published by Our Written Lives, LLC
San Antonio, TX
www.OurWrittenLives.com

Library of Congress Cataloging-in-Publication Data
Hall, Ashley-Lynn
Traveling the Bible: Into the Garden
ISBN: 978-1-942923-87-9

Designed by Sarah Chang
Edited by Sarah Chang and Rachael Hartman

A Note from the Author

I wrote this book so readers could experience
the Bible coming to life from their
perspective. Each chapter has a section for
boys and a section for girls.

In order to allow readers to stay true to their
perspective, I've chosen to use the non-
gendered pronoun "they" when referring to
the friend character in this book.

Dedication

I dedicate this book to Jesus Christ,
my inspiration and my God.

And to my children, who give me the
strength and will to keep going.

And to my church family.
Thank you for being there for us.

into the garden

"Do we seriously have to go to church again, Mom?"

"Yes, we do."

"Why? All of my friends make fun of me."

"That does *not* matter. We are going to church. End of discussion."

"But, Mom–"

"Enough! We are going to church!"

Angry, I stomp to the car and get in, slamming the door just enough so Mom knows my disapproval, but not enough to get in trouble. I buckle up, not wanting to hear another story about how car accidents kill kids. We drive to church, just Mom and I today, since Dad is at work.

I drop into the pew, irritated. Mom gives me a disapproving glance, so I straighten up. I sit there unmoving, my own act of rebellion, as Mom and many others sing songs, give money, and listen attentively to a sermon that seems like a bunch of restrictions on what I can do.

Blah, blah, blah . . . whatever.

The preacher invites people to the front to pray. Many go up to the front, including Mom.

She must enjoy embarrassing me.

I sink down into the pew trying to disappear as I roll my eyes.

I know Mom believes prayer works, but I am not sure I even believe in God. Even if God is out there, why would a perfect being that lives forever care about someone like me? After another song, church is finally over.

Once we are home, Mom mentions my attitude—it's become our Sunday ritual. She tells me to start my weekend chores. I do them, only to avoid having more chores added to the list.

The weeks go on. Every Sunday morning I beg to stay home from church. Every Sunday afternoon, I work on chores around the house. Then, every Sunday evening, Mom sits down to pray in her "prayer chair." I know, you're probably wondering what a "prayer chair" is. It's really just a comfy office chair pulled up to a small table next to a corkboard collage of pink, yellow, and blue sticky notes, and scrap paper of various sizes. That's where she writes all of her prayer requests and answers to prayers she has prayed. Sometimes I sneak a look at what she has up there.

It's too early for dinner, but I am already hungry. I want to ask for a snack, but Mom is kneeling on the floor in front of the prayer chair, a bundle of sticky notes in hand. When she is praying, no one can pay me to interrupt her for anything other than a dire emergency.

After ten minutes of Mom being on her knees, I decide a snack is out of the question. I have no choice but to wait until dinner. I decide to play my favorite video game. I am really into the game, nearly finished with the structure I've been building for weeks, when I hear Mom call out, "Time for dinner!"

With a sigh, I save my progress and go eat. My parents have a strict "you eat what is served when it is served or do without" policy, so I was not about to finish this part

of my game, especially when my stomach has already been growling at me for an hour.

After dinner, Mom asks me to do the dishes. I did so many chores already today, but I know Dad always backs her up, so I just stand up with no complaint to do the dishes as my parents sit at the table chatting about their days.

"How was work today?" Mom asks Dad, as she does every day.

I move my mouth in synchrony as my dad says the same thing he always says, "Absolutely fine, my dear."

I zone out of their conversation as I scrub the brown bits of chicken from the pan. I am quick to listen again when I hear them talking about me. I only catch bits of the conversation now because they are now speaking in hushed tones.

"I'm just concerned . . ."

". . . never asks for a friend to visit . . ."

". . . I've been praying . . ."

Maybe I would have a friend visit if my whole weekend wasn't filled with church and chores.

I don't want to listen to the conversation anymore. I rush to finish the dishes, likely not doing the best job, and hurriedly return to my game upstairs.

...

It's Monday and there is a new kid in school, seated right next to me in homeroom. I introduce myself out of kindness, but something about this person makes me want to talk more.

After several days of talking while the teachers weren't paying attention or griping at us to do our school work, I find I have a lot in common with the new kid. I am still caught by surprise when my new friend asks me to spend the night on Saturday.

I stutter as I say, "My mom makes me go to church on Sundays." I immediately regret it. *What if this kid thinks church isn't cool? I certainly don't think it is.*

I am even more surprised when they respond, "That's fine. My family also goes to church. You could go with us or maybe I could spend the night and go to church with you! We have been trying to find a new home church."

I try to talk my new friend out of the sleepover idea. I'm sure we will not be friends long if I have anyone over, especially overnight. My protest gets me nowhere; this kid is determined to spend time with me outside of school. That afternoon as school gets out, our families meet up in the student pick-up line. My parents seem overjoyed with the idea of me having a friend stay the night.

The plan is made. My friend will come to my house tomorrow and their parents will meet us at church on Sunday morning.

To prevent my parents from having my friend do any chores around my house, I do everything I can think of before Saturday arrives. The last thing I need is to have my friend watching me do chores. Or worse, my parents making my friend do chores.

Just after lunch on Saturday, as I rush to fold the last of my clothes and slam my dresser drawers shut, I hear a car door slam shut. My friend is here!

We spend the afternoon together, having more fun than I've had by myself in months. To my surprise, my parents are actually pleasant at dinner and don't bring up any embarrassing stories. I see my friend has already finished their vegetables, so I force myself to swallow my last piece of cooked broccoli.

Just as I am about to ask if we could be excused from the table, my friend blurts out, "Do you mind if I do the dishes?"

I am astonished. Why would anyone volunteer to do an extra chore?

My parents smile and chuckle. I truly believe they are about to take my friend up on the offer, but instead they tell us to go have fun and they would clean up dinner.

In my room, I ask, "Why would you volunteer to do chores at all, let alone here?"

My friend laughs, "The politer I am to your parents, the more we can hang out outside of school. Plus, at home it gets done faster than griping or complaining about it, so I get more free time. I would rather spend time doing what I enjoy than complaining about what I do not enjoy. What games do you have?"

We play my favorite video game, which happens to also be my friend's favorite game too. When I look at the clock on my nightstand, I realize it is an hour past my usual bedtime. I don't think I've ever felt time move so fast.

I am sleepy the next morning and my friend can read the look on my face when Mom calls us to get ready for church. "Don't argue, you know it won't do any good," my friend says quietly, with a little laugh.

I have to agree.

...

Today's service is another familiar sermon about the oneness of God: the father, the son, and the Holy Spirit.

Apparently, they are all just one God, but it certainly sounds like three to me.

I tap my friend's shoulder to say something, but the only response I get is, "Hush, we need to learn from the pastor."

My face becomes warm like I've been sitting in the sun too long. I silently listen to my friend sing the songs. I stand when everyone stands and sit when everyone sits. This up-and-down service feels like a workout, but I don't want to admit that to my friend.

My friend sings the songs, gives in the offering, and goes to the front to pray at the end of the sermon. Wow, I'm surprised by how into the service my new friend is.

After the service finally ends and we are out of earshot from all the parents, I ask, "Why do you do all that stuff in the service, like singing, praying, and giving?"

My friend smiles and says, "I have seen what God can do. I know what He did for me."

I drop the subject. Obviously this is another person who has their mind made up about God.

After the service, my friend goes home with their parents and I get back into the car with Mom. To my surprise, Mom's first words are, "I like your friend."

Not knowing what to say, I shrug.

Over the next several months, I have my friend over once a month for an "overnight go to church the next day" sleepover. At church, my friend participates while I pretend.

It's not too long before my friend's parents join this church and we sit together every Sunday, even when there isn't a sleepover. I have to admit, having a church friend has sort of gotten to me. I can feel my heart warming to the idea of God just a bit.

After another sleepover weekend is over and while Mom is kneeling and praying at her chair with her sticky notes, I decide to give the prayer thing a try myself–alone in my room, of course! I doubt it will do any good, but I pray: "God, if You exist, prove it to me. Give me an experience I'll never forget."

Boys, continue reading on the next page.
Girls, continue reading on page 18.

Boys, begin reading here.

...

My eyes open, and I wake up more easily than usual. I must have had the best sleep of my life last night. The sunlight wraps me up like a blanket and beams into my eyes. The air around me smells fresh and clean.

As I open my eyes, I realize my bed is nowhere in sight. In fact, I'm not at home anymore. I'm outside, in what looks like a garden.

I see a rabbit hop just in front of me. Slightly startled, I sit up and gaze at everything. There are big, beautiful trees all around me, many full of delicious looking fruit. Animals seem to not fear me; the rabbit and a frog are almost within reach. I see a deer prancing with glee not too far in the distance, and a flutter of happily singing birds among the bright green leaves above me.

I walk slowly and cautiously. This must be a dream, and I want to explore this place like I explore the new places in my video game.

No one seems to be around, so I walk on. I find a river with the coldest water I've ever encountered and take a drink. It's the best water I've ever tasted. I walk by several more animals, including a lion who almost seems to greet me with a smile, but I still keep my distance.

After what feels like several hours, I see a girl in the garden! I quickly turn away and pretend to not notice her by grabbing some fruit to eat. Like the water, it's the best fruit I've ever tasted—apple, pear, or whatever it is.

I hear the girl laugh, "Adam, you have been dreaming again, haven't you?"

She speaks in a language I've never heard before, yet I somehow understand her.

Is she talking to me? I don't see anyone else around here. Why is she calling me Adam?

Since I am the only one around besides the animals, I reply, "Sure. Are we the only ones here?"

She laughs again, "You told me God created you, then formed me from your rib while you were asleep. God gave us this garden to live in. It's just us and God. Let's walk together."

Though I want to keep exploring on my own, I feel an urge to join her. "Alright," I say, "Let's make it a game and pretend I don't know anything, and you tell me everything about this place."

If she goes along with the game, I will not have to explain why I do not know anything about where we are. I wonder what reason I could come up with to explain why I am here. She apparently thinks I am her friend, Adam.

She laughs, "Okay! I love this game."

We walk and talk for hours. Whenever I get hungry, I eat some fruit. Whenever I get thirsty, I find a spring and drink some water. The animals walk with us at times, then run off with their families.

As the sun sets, we find a nice place to sit. I notice Eve is smiling.

"Adam, Eve," a voice calls out. The voice is filled with love and strength. It is soft, yet seems to hold all authority. I am startled, but I want to listen.

"Come walk with Me," the voice says.

We follow and start to talk with the voice. It must be God. It's either God or some advanced alien life form that has learned the language of this strange place. For all I know, I could have been kidnapped by aliens while I slept and put into some hologram program.

We talk about our day and share our experience in the garden. God asks us different kinds of questions than our parents ever do. It's almost like He wants to get to know us and not just find something to punish us for.

After a day in the garden, I drift back into sleep under a sky filled with more stars than I have ever seen.

Continue reading on page 23.

Girls, begin reading here.

...

My eyes open, and I wake up more easily than usual. I must have had the best sleep of my life last night. The sunlight wraps me up like a blanket and beams into my eyes. The air around me smells fresh and clean.

As I open my eyes, I realize my bed is nowhere in sight. In fact, I'm not at home anymore. I'm outside, in what looks like a garden.

I see a rabbit hop just in front of me. Slightly startled, I sit up and gaze at everything. There are big, beautiful trees all around me, many full of delicious-looking fruit. Animals don't seem to fear me; the rabbit and a frog are almost within reach. I see a deer prancing with glee not too far in the distance, and a flutter of happily singing birds among the bright green leaves above me.

I walk slowly and cautiously. This must be a dream, and I want to explore this place like I explore the new places in my video game.

No one seems to be around, so I walk on. I find a river with the coldest water I've ever encountered and take a drink. It's the best water I've ever tasted. I walk by several more animals, including a lion who almost seems to greet me with a smile, but I still keep my distance.

After what feels like several hours, I see a boy in the garden! I quickly turn away and pretend not to notice him by grabbing some fruit to eat. Like the water, it's the best fruit I've ever tasted—apple, pear, or whatever it is.

The boy smiles and waves at me.

Unsure who the boy thinks I am, I ask, "Can you tell me where we are? How did we get here?"

He laughs, "We are where God placed me and made you. We are in the garden, in Eden, remember?"

To that, I say, "Remind me . . . Remind me about everything."

"You already know everything!" he laughed.

I couldn't help but smile back at him. "Well, pretend I don't know anything. We'll make it a game."

"Alright," he says. "God made me from the dust and gave me the breath of life. Then He placed me here in Eden. After that, He told me to name everything. Once I did, I went to sleep. When I woke up, God led you to me. He told me you were formed from my rib. We are the only people in the garden."

Stuck on one thing he said, I ask, "Where is this person you call God?"

He looks puzzled, "What do you mean person? God is not like us. He is all around us." I must look confused, because he continues. "God walks and talks with us in the evenings. You will hear him then."

I figure he is done on the subject, so I say, "You never told me your name?"

He replies, "Adam."

I ask, "How old are we?"

Adam laughs, "I have not counted. Want to walk in the garden together, Eve?"

I was startled when he called me Eve. Unsure if I really want to walk, I shrug. He walks off without me, and I decide to run and catch up. He shows me a small pond I had not noticed when I explored earlier.

The water is very clear, so I look closer. I see many fish, but I also see Adam's reflection, the reflection of all the plants and animals nearby, and what must be my own reflection, or rather the one Adam calls Eve.

She sort of looks like me. At least her hair color is the same, but her eyes are shaped differently than mine.

We continue our walk. Whenever I get hungry, I eat some fruit. Whenever I get thirsty, I find a spring and drink some water. The animals walk with us at times, then run off with their families.

As the sun sets, we find a nice place to sit. I notice Adam is smiling, though I still try not to look too much in his direction.

"Adam, Eve," a voice calls out. The voice is filled with love and strength. It is soft, yet seems to hold all authority. Though startled, I want to hear what the voice says.

"Come walk with me."

We follow and start to talk with the voice. It must be God. It's either God or some advanced alien life form that has learned the language of this strange place. For all I know, I could have been kidnapped by aliens while I slept and put into some hologram program.

We talk about our day and share our experience in the garden. God asks us different kinds of questions than our parents ever do. It's almost like He wants to get to know us and not just find something to punish us for.

After a day in the garden, I drift back into sleep under a sky filled with more stars than I have ever seen.

Continue reading on page 23.

Chapter Two

something about that dream

At breakfast, I tell my family about my dream.

"Very interesting," Mom sets my plate at the table and turns back towards the kitchen sink. She doesn't seem to fully grasp the experience I had.

"It felt so real," I continued.

Dad smiles, "Sometimes dreams do feel real. Sounds like you went on quite the journey!"

"I did!" I'm glad Dad seems to understand. "I explored this whole land, and there was another kid there too, but it was someone I had never seen before. They said God placed us there."

Mom's interest piques at my statement about God. She looks at me with a smile on her face and adds, "And God gave you both a purpose."

It's no surprise that she turns my moment into another Bible lesson.

"Go get ready. We need to get into the car and get you to school," Mom says.

...

It's Saturday, and my friend comes over. Now that we are alone, without our classmates surrounding us, I can finally tell my friend about my dream.

My friend smiles, strangely in the same way Mom did at breakfast yesterday morning. "My mom has a thing with dreams. She says that the dreams that feel real, the ones that we can't stop thinking about, those are the dreams God gives us for a reason."

I roll my eyes. "I don't believe in God, remember?"

My friend sticks out their tongue, then says, "Well, I will believe enough for the both of us." Letting out a little laugh, they ask, "Was there anything else that happened in your dream?"

"No, we just walked around this really beautiful place. I think the other person called it Eden."

My friend looks at me like they know something I don't.

"What?" I ask, drawing out the word as I roll my eyes.

"Nothing." My friend has a smirk on their face. "I was just thinking about what it could mean."

"Tell me!"

"No, let me think about it more. It just reminds me of something."

I can tell my friend is keeping something from me, but I don't push the conversation. I just want to continue exploring the video game world we started our last sleepover. We explore and slowly build our kingdom out of square, gray blocks.

The day goes by fast and Sunday morning comes even quicker.

Church, as usual, is kind of boring for me, but I am singing some of the songs with my friend now. I struggle to understand the sermon, but my friend smiles and nods their head with everyone else.

Honestly, I don't think I will ever understand what the pastor means by the things he says.

I swing my feet in the pew until Mom sets her hand on my leg, the signal for me to stop. I let out a sigh and stare forward, allowing my mind to wander until everyone stands up to sing the final song.

After church, my friend and I walk to the foyer with our families. We stand there and talk for another hour or so. It's not really an hour, but it certainly feels like it.

An older man, someone I have never noticed before, approaches us, interrupting our conversation. "God told me one of you asked for an unforgettable experience. Always remember, God hears you." The man winks, my friend politely smiles, and I try to keep my face from sharing the strange feeling I have inside.

"That was weird," I say nervously after the man leaves.

"I wonder who he was talking about?" My friend asks sarcastically. They give me the same look they gave me last night when they wouldn't tell me what they knew about my dream.

I feel stressed, like I'm being put on the spot, but I'm doing my best not to show it.

The pastor comes over and greets us. "How is everyone doing?"

The way he asks the question makes me wonder: *does he know about my dream too?*

"I see y'all were talking to my old friend. A very wise man, isn't he?" the pastor says nodding in the direction of the old man.

Our parents begin talking about how wonderful it was to meet him. They share how he said something about an "unforgettable experience."

The pastor leans in, obviously intrigued by the statement. "He is very close with God. Talks to our Father more than anyone I know—including myself!" he chuckles. "I'd keep close to what he says. He's delivered many messages from God Himself."

I feel a resistance welling up inside of me. I do *not* want to believe the old man talks with God. I open my mouth and say the first thing that pops out. "Pastor, you say you believe in one God, but you talk as if there are three?"

My mother gasps. I know she's going to say something about "backtalk" on the car ride home. I know I said it with an attitude, but it was a genuine question just the same.

The pastor doesn't seem to mind what I said. He responds with a reassuring calm tone. "That's a misconception. You see, there are not three gods. There is only one God. Depending on the situation, God can show up in different ways. We see Him often as the Holy Spirit who lives in our hearts. He is also Jesus, who came to Earth to help everyone and free us from our sins. He is also the loving Father who created everything—every person, animal, and plant we see. Make sense?"

Still not understanding most of his response, I ask, "Can God tell us what dreams mean?"

The pastor smiles, pleased by my curiosity, "If you listen, He can. He has even given people the gift to interpret dreams. I'm not one of the lucky ones with that gift though."

As the pastor leaves, my friend turns to me, "I've been thinking more about your dream. I think you need to read your Bible. Start in Genesis."

"Seriously? That's all you've got?" I look my friend in the eye, challenging them. Reading the Bible is the last thing I want to do. Why can't my friend just tell me what my dream means?

My friend doesn't take the challenge, "Suit yourself. I just know you would find it interesting."

. . .

That evening, as I lay in bed still thinking about my dream, I whisper to my bedroom wall, "God does not exist. I have not had an unforgettable experience. A dream is not an unforgettable experience."

Boys, continue reading on the next page.
Girls, continue reading on page 33.

Boys, begin reading here.

...

I wake up in the garden again. Nothing has changed and everything is perfect.

Eve is reaching for the fruit from a tree. She hops, grabs it, and turns towards me, "Morning, Adam! Would you like something to eat?" She sure is cheerful.

"Okay," I say, squinting as my eyes adjust to the brightness of the sun. The sun in my dreams seems a lot brighter than the normal sun.

I must look confused or something, because Eve looks at me with concern on her face, "Feeling down again, Adam?"

"I guess," I reply, "I just slept a little funny." I think about telling her about how this is all a dream, and how it bothers me, but something about being in the garden makes me feel at peace. As quickly as my troubles come over me, they are lifted. I stand up and take the fruit from her hand.

We walk together, admiring the animals and the trees. Though Eve lives in the garden, she seems just as awestruck as I am when I point out something new.

I get along with her better than any friend I've ever had, and I don't feel a need to hide my thoughts or feelings. We laugh as the birds chase each other. I'm not even startled when I see a mother bear roll on the ground in front of me with her cub.

Eve asks a question that has been on my mind, "Do you ever think about what life would be like outside of the garden?"

I answer honestly, "This place is better than anywhere else. This place is perfect. Everything here is beautiful. We have a perfect friendship. There's no pain or sadness, and there's an overwhelming peace everywhere I go."

Eve jumps with joy and says, "God is peace!"

Here, in this dream, I don't feel a need to argue or roll my eyes. I agree with her. God is peace!

As we continue walking, Eve stops and looks at a pair of trees in the center of an opening in the garden, "Do you ever wonder about the fruit on the tree?"

"Those trees?" I point to the two beautiful trees, full of a fruit I have never seen before. The fruit looks good, but something inside of me says not to touch it.

"Curiosity is something God gave us, but let's keep walking. We can't eat that fruit anyway."

Eve grabs my hand, pulling me away from the tree toward a field of flowers. Some of the flowers are colors I have never seen before.

"Remind me, Eve," I say, stopping her before we distract ourselves with the beauty surrounding us, "Why can't we have that fruit?"

Eve looks at me seriously and drops her voice to nearly whisper, "If we eat that fruit, God told us we will die."

"Okay," I say. I don't want to test that. I tag Eve's arm and begin running through the flowers, "I'll race you!"

We run and laugh through the meadow. The bees race with us and the birds chirp to cheer us on.

We enjoy everything the garden has to offer. That evening, I hear my name called from the skies above. Is God talking to me?

I smile. It has to be God, and I'm so excited He is talking to *me*.

Continue reading on page 37.

Girls, begin reading here.

...

I wake up in the garden again. Nothing has changed and everything is perfect.

Adam is reaching for the fruit from a tree. He hops, grabs it, and turns towards me. "Morning, Eve! Would you like something to eat?" He sure is cheerful.

"Okay," I say, squinting as my eyes adjust to the brightness of the sun. The sun in my dreams seems a lot brighter than the normal sun.

I must look confused or something, because Adam looks at me with concern on his face, "Feeling down again, Eve?"

"I guess," I reply, "I just slept a little funny." I think about telling him about how this is all a dream, and how it bothers me, but something about being in the garden makes me feel at peace. As quickly as my troubles come over me, they are lifted. I stand up and take the fruit from his hand.

We walk together, admiring the animals and the trees. Though Adam lives in the garden, he seems just as awestruck as I am when I point out something new. I get along with him better than any friend I've ever had, and don't feel a need to hide my thoughts or feelings. We laugh as the birds chase each other. I'm not even startled when I see a mother bear roll on the ground in front of me with her cub.

Adam asks a question that has been on my mind, "Do you ever think about what life would be outside of the garden?"

I answer honestly, "This place is better than anywhere else. This place is perfect. Everything here is beautiful. We have a perfect friendship. There's no pain or sadness, and there's an overwhelming peace everywhere I go."

Adam jumps with joy and says, "God is peace!"

Here, in this dream, I don't feel a need to argue or roll my eyes. I agree with him. God is peace!

As we continue walking, Adam stops and looks at a pair of trees in the center of an opening in the garden, "Do you ever wonder about the fruit on the tree?"

"Those trees?" I point to the two beautiful trees, full of a fruit I have never seen before. The fruit looks good, but something inside of me says not to touch it.

"Curiosity is something God gave us, but let's keep walking. We can't eat that fruit anyway."

Adam grabs my hand, pulling me away from the tree toward a field of flowers. Some of the flowers are colors I have never seen before.

"Remind me, Adam," I say, stopping him before we distract ourselves with the beauty surrounding us, "Why can't we have that fruit?"

Adam looks at me seriously and drops his voice to nearly whisper, "If we eat that fruit, God told us we will die."

"Okay," I say. I don't want to test that. I tag Adam's arm and begin running through the flowers, "I'll race you!"

We run and laugh through the meadow. The bees race with us and the birds chirp to cheer us on.

We enjoy everything the garden has to offer. That evening, I hear my name called from the skies above. Is God talking to me?

I smile. It has to be God, and I'm so excited He is talking to me.

Continue reading on page 37.

Chapter Three
the garden in the book

It's Saturday, and my alarm clock silently stares at me as sun rays gently nudge me awake. I stretch, enjoying the quiet moment and the comfort of my bed. I don't have any homework, and the weather is beautiful. Breakfast is calling my name. I get out of bed and dress for the day, putting on a casual outfit, socks, and tennis shoes.

Mom greets me with a smile as I enter the kitchen. "Good morning!" she says, sounding chipper.

"Good morning," I respond, not as chipper, but I smile back.

"Your dad and I are both off today, so we thought we'd make it a family day. First, grab something to eat. Then, we'll go to the park," she says.

"Sounds good to me."

Mom hands me an apple and a granola bar. "After the park, we'll go out for lunch, so this should be enough until then."

We don't waste any time heading to the car. The park is only ten minutes away. When we arrive, Dad heads off to jog around the lake. I jump on a swing, and Mom walks to a nearby picnic table with her book.

Lightly rocking, I look around. The sky is blue, and the breeze is crisp. There are a couple of old, large trees not too far from me. They provide some shade from the spring sun, but there isn't anything special about them. In the distance, I see more green—grass, bushes, and trees—but nothing as vibrant as what I've seen in my dreams. A few pink flowers grow between the sidewalk and the road, but they don't compare to the rainbow fields full of perfect blooms I see while I sleep.

Two hours later, we get back in the car and head to the restaurant for an early lunch. It's a small place with good food and low prices—a family favorite. I order a burger and fries. As I eat, I miss the sweet, crisp fruits from the garden. The food in the real world doesn't compare to the flavorful and fresh treats I experience in my dream.

Next, we stop at the library. My parents know exactly what books they want to check out. Mom still has a few chapters left in the book she was reading earlier, so she sits down to finish her novel.

I walk through the aisles, looking at all the titles. Overwhelmed by the thousands of books around me, I think of what my friend said: "You need to read Genesis."

I usually play video games, but tonight, I choose to open my Bible instead. I don't remember the last time I opened it—maybe the day my parents bought it for me.

I start reading:

> **Genesis 1:1-2** – *In the beginning, God created the heavens and the earth. Now the earth was formless and empty, darkness covered the surface of the watery depths, and the Spirit of God was hovering over the surface of the waters.*

I notice it mentions the Spirit of God, just like the pastor was talking about last Sunday.

I skip to the next page.

> **Genesis 2:8-9** – *The Lord God planted a garden in Eden, in the east, and there he placed the man he had formed. 9 The Lord God caused to grow out of the ground every tree pleasing in appearance and good for food, including the tree of life in the middle of the garden, as well as the tree of the knowledge of good and evil.*

I keep reading. I feel overwhelmed with surprise. It's describing the garden from my dreams! Everything is the same—down to the name of the garden and the names of the people. I'm reading the story of Adam and Eve in the Garden of Eden, but I know it so well because I've lived it.

I reread those verses. My eyes grow heavy and I drift off to sleep.

Boys, continue reading on the next page.
Girls, continue reading on page 45.

Boys, begin reading here.

. . .

"Eden really is a remarkable place," I say as Eve and I go about our usual tending to the garden. She agrees with me. We gather fruit, vegetables, and flowers, removing the harvest so younger blooms get the sunlight they need to grow. Unlike doing chores at home, I am eager to gather our daily food, and help maintain the beauty of the garden.

The day is bright and I feel the sun hugging my skin. "Let's go to the stream." After all of the work, I am ready for a drink of water.

"You go," she says with a smile, "I'll meet you in the center of the garden. I want to rest in the shade of the great trees."

I nod with excitement and we go our separate ways.

I follow the path to the stream. The water trickles and splashes around the rocks, making music the frogs croak along to. A fish tries to make its way upstream and I let out a laugh. The water tastes perfect.

I stroll to the center of the garden and see Eve standing at one of the trees God strictly forbade us to eat from. She is holding a piece of fruit from the Tree of the Knowledge of Good and Evil, and talking to someone. But who? Before I reach her, she takes a bite of the fruit.

"Eve!" I shout and she glances over to me with a big smile. "What are you doing?" For the first time in this place, I am panicking.

"Adam," she says with delight in her eyes. "I tasted the fruit and it is good. Try some!"

She holds the fruit out for me to take. "Won't we die if we eat it?" I am hesitant to grab it from her hand, but unlike me, she isn't panicked.

"Adam, I ate the fruit and I did not die," Eve says sincerely.

"Believe me," a serpent that clung to the tree spoke to us. "God does not want you to eat this fruit because He knows when you eat it you will be like Him, and He does not want that. Your eyes will open and you will see and know what is good and what is evil."

I take the fruit from Eve's hands. Seeing she is still alive, I decide to eat some as well. This fruit tastes different from the others in the garden.

I immediately feel my face become red and hot. My heart drops into the pit of my stomach. I look up at Eve, but she won't look me in the eyes. A strong breeze moves through the garden. I shiver and I feel little bumps on my skin. Something about this garden doesn't feel right anymore. I don't want to be seen, so we hide in the trees.

"Adam, Eve," I hear God's voice call for us. This time, I hear the same tone of disappointment I hear from my parents when I get in trouble. We don't move from our hiding spots.

"Where are you?" God calls out again. This time we slowly reveal ourselves to stand before God.

I speak first. "I was afraid, so I hid."

"Have you eaten from the tree which I commanded you not to eat?" He already knew the answer.

"Yes," I whisper with my head down, "Eve handed me fruit from the tree, and I ate."

Next, God speaks to Eve, "What have you done?" He sounds sad.

Eve speaks, like me, nearly whispering. "The serpent tricked me, and I ate the fruit."

Angry, God speaks to the serpent, "Because you have done this, you are cursed more than any other creature. You will crawl on your belly and eat dirt all of your life."

The serpent tricked us, but he didn't eat the fruit. This garden wasn't for him. I fear the punishment God will give us.

To Eve, God says, "In your future, you will have pain and worries when you become pregnant and in childbirth. Your husband will rule over you."

God then speaks to me, "Adam, because you listened to Eve and ate the fruit I told you not to eat, you will work and sweat all your life to provide food for your family. The ground will have thorns and thistles, weeds, and dead things you will have to deal with. You came from dust and you will return to dust when you die."

I whisper, "I'm sorry."

God leads us out of the garden, into a vast wilderness. He tells us we will never return to beautiful Eden.

We look back as we leave the garden and see a powerful, winged person swinging a flaming sword back and forth, guarding us from coming back into the garden. I know it is impossible to go back.

I feel we will eventually die out here in the wild. That must be what God meant when he said if we ate from the forbidden fruit we would surely die. We both have a lot on our minds, but Eve and I curl up in a small cave and go to sleep.

Continue reading on page 51.

Girls, begin reading here.

…

"Eden really is a remarkable place," I say as Adam and I go about our usual tending to the garden. He agrees with me. We gather fruit, vegetables, and flowers, removing the harvest so younger blooms get the sunlight they need to grow. Unlike doing chores at home, I am eager to gather our daily food, and help maintain the beauty of the garden.

The day is bright and I feel the sun hugging my skin. "Let's go to the stream," Adam suggests. After all of the work, I can tell he is ready to splash some cool water on his face.

"You go," I say with a smile. "I'll meet you in the center of the garden. I want to rest in the shade of the great trees."

Adam nods with excitement and we go our separate ways.

I follow the path deeper into the garden. The trees around me dance to the songs birds sing as they fly in the sky. A cricket chirps a melody in tune with the breeze and the ripple of the creek in the distance.

In the center of the garden are the trees God told us not to touch. They are the biggest trees around, the most beautiful, their shade is the coolest spot to rest, and the grass around them is softer than the most comforting feather bed you can imagine.

As I sink down into the grass, I see a serpent slither around the bottom trunk of one of the trees. The snake rises tall so his eyes level with mine.

"Hello, Eve. Resting comfortably?

I didn't answer. The fact that the creature is talking does not surprise me, but something about his voice does. It does not seem to match the beauty of this place.

"Didn't God say you could eat from any tree in the garden?" He hissed.

"Yes, we can eat from any tree in the garden," I tell him, "but God said we cannot eat fruit from these two trees in the middle of the garden—the Tree of Life, and the Tree of the Knowledge of Good and Evil—or we will die."

The serpent let out a laugh, "You won't die! God does not want you to eat this fruit because He knows when you eat it you will be like Him, and He does not want that. Your eyes will open and you will see and know what is good and what is evil."

I look at the fruit on the tree. I've been working all day and I am hungry. The fruit looks really good. Perhaps, one bite won't be a problem. After all, God provided all the food in the garden for us to eat.

I take a bite. It tastes different from the other fruit I've had in the garden.

"Eve!" I hear Adam shout behind me, and I turn toward him and smile. "What are you doing?" he shouts. For the first time in this place, I see Adam panicking.

"Adam," I say with delight in my eyes, "I tasted the fruit and it is good. Try some!" I hold the fruit out toward him.

"Won't we die if we eat it?" He seems hesitant to grab it from my hand, but I want him to try it with me.

"Adam, I ate the fruit and I did not die," I say sincerely.

"Believe me," the serpent says to us, "You will know everything, just like God."

Seeing I am still alive, Adam takes the fruit from my hand. After he takes a bite, I immediately feel my face become red and hot. My heart drops into the pit of my stomach. I look up at Adam, but he won't look me in the eyes. A strong breeze moves through the garden. I shiver and I feel little bumps on my skin. Something about the garden doesn't feel right anymore. I don't want to be seen, so we hide among the trees.

"Adam, Eve," I hear God's voice call for us. This time, I hear the same tone of disappointment I hear from my parents when I get in trouble. We don't move from our hiding spots.

"Where are you?" God calls out again. This time we slowly reveal ourselves to stand before God.

Adam speaks out, "I was afraid, so I hid."

"Have you eaten from the tree which I commanded you not to eat?" He already knew the answer.

"Yes," Adam whispers with his head down. "Eve handed me fruit from the tree, and I ate."

Next, God spoke to me. "What have you done?" He sounds sad.

I speak, like Adam, nearly whispering. "The serpent tricked me, and I ate the fruit."

Angry, God speaks to the serpent, "Because you have done this, you are cursed more than any other creature. You will crawl on your belly and eat dirt all of your life."

The serpent tricked us, but he didn't eat the fruit. This garden wasn't for him. I fear the punishment God will give us.

To me, God says, "In your future, you will have pain and worries when you become pregnant and in childbirth. Your husband will rule over you."

God then speaks to Adam, "Adam, because you listened to Eve and ate the fruit I told you not to eat, you will work and sweat all your life to provide food for your family. The ground will have thorns and thistles, weeds, and dead things you will have to deal with. You came from dust and you will return to dust when you die."

I whisper, "I'm sorry."

God leads us out of the garden, into a vast wilderness. He tells us we will never return to beautiful Eden.

We look back as we leave the garden and see a powerful, winged person swinging a flaming sword back and forth, guarding us from coming back into the garden. I know it is impossible to go back.

I feel we will eventually die out here in the wild. That must be what God meant when he said if we ate from the forbidden fruit we would surely die. We both have a lot on our minds, but Adam and I curl up in a small cave and go to sleep.

Continue reading on page 51.

Chapter Four

a creation made to explore

I wake up in my bed at home. I am no longer sure if my life with my parents is reality, or if the garden and our banishment are what's real.

In a daze, I slowly walk to the kitchen for breakfast. Mom is making pancakes for me. I cut a piece with my fork. Looking up at Mom and Dad, I ask, "What day is it?"

"Friday," Dad replies quickly.

"Better finish eating; you don't want to miss the bus," Mom adds.

I accept that I am living in reality and continue to eat my breakfast. Time moves fast, as it seems to magically do every morning, and I make it to the end of my driveway just as the bus pulls up.

On the ride to school, and while sitting at my desk in my homeroom class, I can't help but think about my dream. In my mind, I clearly see the large winged person with the flaming sword.

The bell rings and I follow the herd of other students into the hall, making my way to math. I stare out the window and watch the trees as their leaves rustle with each little gust of wind. It reminds me of the garden where the trees dance in tune with the rest of nature.

In science class, my teacher says something about water cycles. I think of the streams of water that trickle through Eden and how cold and refreshing the water is. Will I ever see the garden again? I wonder.

At lunch, I sit quietly with my friend as they start listing all the things we can do this weekend. Since I am not acknowledging what they are saying, my friend turns to me and asks, "Are you okay?"

"No," I sigh. "I had another dream last night."

My friend looks at me with their full attention. "Tell me about it. What happened?"

I tell them about harvesting in the garden, the talking serpent, and the winged creature with the fiery sword. "I just feel a little lost. I don't know why I keep thinking about it. Sometimes I can't tell if it is just a dream, or if it's reality and us being here at school is the dream."

My friend smiles and says, "I have two thoughts. First, losing track of who you are is expected in the process of learning who you are."

"That makes no sense," I protest, "and you kind of sound like the pastor."

We both laugh. My friend points their finger and makes a face like the pastor does when he makes a good point, and we laugh even more. I realize laughter is what I need to feel more like myself again.

We calm down and return to our lunches. "What's your second thought?" I ask my friend.

My friend laughs a little more, then begins to speak again, "Second—"

The bell rings. Lunch is over.

"I'll tell you after school."

My friend grabs their lunch tray and heads toward the trash. I follow.

"Why not now?"

My friend smiles at me. I hear the roar of middle school students growing louder as everyone makes their way toward the hall.

"After school," my friend reassures me.

The rest of that day, I am more attentive in class. I take notes, ask questions, and write down each homework assignment. When the bell rings at the end of the school day, I rush back to each of my morning classes to apologize for not paying attention and to ask the teachers what the homework assignment is.

I rush toward the bus just as my bus driver is closing the door. She sees me, gives me a knowing look, and opens the door for me. Out of breath, I plop into the seat next to my friend. I nearly missed the bus twice today. Normally, we ride different buses home, but this weekend my friend's parents wanted to go out of town, so they are riding home with me for a two-night sleepover. The bus jolts forward. We embrace the thump-thump as it rolls over the speed bumps to exit the parking lot.

My friend turns toward me, "Did you want to hear my second thought from earlier today?"

"Yes," I say, pushing my backpack to my feet, giving us more space and making the seat comfortable.

"Have you read Genesis yet?"

I hesitate, but answer truthfully. "I started to, but didn't finish. It was weird how it described everything I dreamed about, even the names."

"I think—" my friend looks me in the eyes with all seriousness. They whisper, "I think you are time traveling into the Bible."

"That's ridiculous!" I say loudly, then lower my tone so other students won't pay attention. "Are you crazy? Time travel?"

"It only makes sense," my friend starts to explain, "You prayed an honest prayer. God loves us being honest with Him and open to miracles in our lives."

"Yeah, but—" I start to respond, but can't think of anything else to say.

"Finish reading Genesis," my friend says earnestly. "It will give you another perspective on your dreams. I think it will help you better understand."

"We have different opinions on that subject. I understand perfectly. I lived it. I don't need to read it again."

The bus pulls up to my driveway, so we drop the subject, grab our backpacks, and step off the bus. The sun is bright and though I can't see them, I hear birds chirping somewhere in the distance.

"Maybe this weekend, we can spend some time outside," I say, staring up at the thin and strangely fast-moving clouds.

"That's a great idea!"

Boys, continue reading on the next page.
Girls, continue reading on page 61.

Boys, begin reading here.

…

I hear the sound of children laughing. Opening my eyes, I see Eve holding the hands of two young boys. They are quickly running in a circle. They move faster and faster, until their hands let go and they all fall toward the ground with more laughter.

Before coming back here, I feared the banishment of my last dream. This, however, is a pleasant sight to wake up to.

One of the boys runs toward me, arms wide, ready to embrace me in a hug. He is maybe four years old. His head comes only to my waist.

"Cain," Eve calls out.

The child, filled with energy, looks toward her.

"Try to catch Abel and me!"

Cain and Abel, I think to myself, making sure to remember the names. Then I join in on the fun. We run, play, and wander around, exploring the new land until the young boys become tired.

Lying in the grass, I notice birds are chirping somewhere in the distance. In Eden, the birds would come right to us and sing their songs. Now, they hide from us, like they do in my real life. I still listen, enjoying their tunes.

"Tell me a story," Cain mutters. I can tell he is exhausted from the fun of the day.

"Eve," I say as I glance at her. "Can you tell us a story?"

"Sure!" She seems happy to share. "What story would you like to hear?"

"World!" Abel says. He is very young and still learning to speak. Abel moves closer to me and lays his head on my lap.

"I love that story!" Eve is genuinely delighted to share the story of how God made the world around us.

She tells the boys about how God created the sky, water, and land, the sun, moon, and stars, every bird and every fish, and all of the creatures on land. She pauses, looks at me and says, "Then God made Adam and God made me. He said it was all very good."

I smile at her. Thinking of Eden makes my heart feel heavy. I wish I could visit the garden once again and see all of its beauty.

Around us, the trees stand tall and fluffy clouds dot the sky. The sun, high above us, spreads a warm light across the earth, sparkling its gold on everything. Flowers reach up as if to grab the sun's rays, bees bounce from one bright petal to another, and butterflies flutter above them. Earth is still beautiful, even though it's not Eden.

I notice a deer in the field. We make eye contact and it immediately leaps away from us. I miss the way animals would trust us in Eden. Now, it seems they sense something wrong and hide themselves.

As Eve combs her fingers through Cain's hair, she continues her story. "On the seventh, God rested and declared all of His creation as holy."

Once the boys are sleeping, Eve whispers, "I know we had a lot of fun today, but we still need to get our work done."

With the boys in her sight, Eve gathers berries from bushes and I pull weeds from the ground. Unlike in Eden, I feel no joy in the tasks we are doing. It feels more like the chores Mom makes me do at home. Hours go by. My back hurts from bending over. My hands are scratched and bleeding from the rough weeds, and I can't seem to catch my breath. There's so much more to do. The sun sits lower in the sky and the air starts to grow cold. I realize I never felt cold in Eden. I shiver.

Eve comes to where I am in the field. "Come with me, I started a fire." I follow her to a nearby small cave where Cain and Abel are sitting. Eve carefully sets up a stick over the flame. A small, gray fish is speared through the middle and rests above the fire, held in place by two forked branches on either side.

My stomach rumbles. I sit between the boys and grab a few berries. Eve rotates the fish over the fire.

The boys lean into me for warmth. I put an arm around both of them. My heart suddenly swells up and I feel the urge to cry, but I hold it in. I am probably just tired or hungry from all the work we did today.

Glancing at Eve, I can tell she feels the same way. We know why we cannot go back, but we both miss the joy and peace of our garden, Eden.

Now, this is our life: farming, gathering, surviving, and caring for these two young boys.

I lie down. Other than the orange glow of the small fire, there seems to be no more color. My eyes grow heavy and I can no longer fight the sleep that washes over me.

Continue on page 67.

Girls, begin reading here.

…

I hear the sound of children laughing. Opening my eyes, I see Adam holding the hands of two young boys. They are quickly running in a circle. They move faster and faster, until their hands let go and they all fall toward the ground with more laughter.

Before coming back here, I feared the banishment of my last dream. This, however, is a pleasant sight to wake up to.

One of the boys runs toward me, arms wide, ready to embrace me in a hug. He is maybe four years old. His head comes only to my waist.

"Cain," Adam calls out.

The child, filled with energy, looks toward him.

"Try to catch Abel and me!"

Cain and Abel, I think to myself, making sure to remember the names. Then I join in on the fun. We run, play, and wander around, exploring the new land until the young boys become tired.

Lying in the grass, I notice birds are chirping somewhere in the distance. In Eden, the birds would come right to us and sing their songs. Now, they hide from us, like they do in my real life. I still listen, enjoying their tunes.

"Tell me a story," Cain mutters. I can tell he is exhausted from the fun of the day.

"Adam," I say as I glance at him. "Can you tell us a story?"

"Sure!" He seems happy to share. "What story would you like to hear?"

"World!" Abel says. He is very young and still learning to speak. Abel moves closer to me and lays his head on my lap.

"I love that story!" Adam is genuinely delighted to share the story of how God made the world around us.

He tells the boys about how God created the sky, water, and land, the sun, moon, and stars, every bird and every fish, and all of the creatures on land. He pauses, looks at me and says, "Then God made me and God made Eve. He said it was all very good."

I smile at him. Thinking of Eden makes my heart feel heavy. I wish I could visit the garden once again and see all of its beauty.

Around us, the trees stand tall and fluffy clouds dot the sky. The sun, high above us, spreads a warm light across the earth, sparkling its gold on everything. Flowers reach up as if to grab the sun's rays, bees bounce from one bright petal to another, and butterflies flutter above them. Earth is still beautiful, even though it's not Eden.

I notice a deer in the field. We make eye contact and it immediately leaps away from us. I miss the way animals would trust us in Eden. Now, it seems they sense something wrong and hide themselves.

I comb my fingers through Cain's hair, as Adam continues the story. "On the seventh, God rested and declared all of His creation as holy."

Once the boys are sleeping, Adam whispers, "I know we had a lot of fun today, but we still need to get our work done."

With the boys in my sight, I begin to gather berries from bushes and Adam pulls weeds from the ground. Unlike in Eden, I feel no joy in the tasks we are doing. It feels more like the chores Mom makes me do at home.

Hours go by. My back hurts from bending over. My hands are scratched and bleeding from the rough weeds, and I can't seem to catch my breath. There's so much more to do. The sun sits lower in the sky and the air starts to grow cold. I realize I never felt cold in Eden. I shiver.

Adam comes to where I am in the bushes. "Come with me, I started a fire."

I follow him to a nearby small cave where Cain and Abel are sitting. He hands the boys the small, handwoven basket of berries I picked.

Adam carefully sets up a stick over the flame. A small, gray fish is speared through the middle and rests above the fire, held in place by two forked branches on either side.

My stomach rumbles. I sit between the boys and grab a few berries. Adam rotates the fish over the fire.

The boys lean into me for warmth. I put an arm around both of them. My heart suddenly swells up and I feel the urge to cry, but I hold it in. I am probably just tired or hungry from all the work we did today.

Glancing at Adam, I can tell he feels the same way. We know why we cannot go back, but we both miss the joy and peace of our garden, Eden.

Now, this is our life: farming, gathering, surviving, and caring for these two young boys.

I lie down. Other than the orange glow of the small fire, there seems to be no more color. My eyes grow heavy and I can no longer fight the sleep that washes over me.

Continue on page 67.

Chapter Five

up in the trees

I wake up and notice my pillow is damp. Am I crying? Or did I drool?

"Finally!" My friend rolls over in their sleeping bag on the air mattress and says, "You slept in so late!"

I wipe the dampness from my face.

"Did you drool?" My friend smirks at me.

"Uh." Not wanting to admit I am waking up crying, I agree. "Yeah."

We both laugh.

I'm exhausted this morning, and too tired to explain why, so I push myself to act normal.

We go downstairs and Mom has breakfast waiting for us. "About time you sleepyheads!" She unwraps the foil from around the pancakes. The way the foil slopes over the plate reminds me of the cave from my dream.

"What's the plan for today?" Mom asks both of us.

My friend, who has much more energy than I do, announces, "We are going to explore outside."

"That sounds like a lot of fun!" Mom loves the idea of us not being in the house. "Explore all you want, but promise me you will stay in the neighborhood and stay safe."

"We will, Mom."

The thought of being outside seems exhausting. I spent all night doing chores in my dream, simply to survive. I want to stay in and play video games, but I already said yes to spending time outside.

My friend and I walk down the street toward our neighborhood park.

"Can you believe this is our last sleepover before summer break?"

I kick a rock that is in my path on the sidewalk. "I know; I'm really excited."

"We can spend more time outside in creation once we don't have to be in school anymore," my friend says.

"In creation? Don't you mean in God's creation?" I blurt out my questions a little more quickly than I intended. I was thinking about Cain and Abel's bedtime story from my dream.

"Of course," my friend says and smiles as if I had asked the question kindly. "I think God's creation is great. I love being outside and seeing all He has created."

I nod my head. My dreams have given me a new love for the outdoors. I feel the closest to being in Eden when I am surrounded by nature. Listening to the birds, appreciating the flowers, and noticing all the little things.

"Look," I point at a tree near the edge of the park. "That tree is perfect for climbing!"

As if on cue, we both run to the tree and grab hold of the limb nearest the ground. I propel myself up first and then help my friend.

"Did you have another dream last night?"

I look at my friend curiously. "How did you know?"

"You've been quiet this morning, like you were yesterday. Here's what I think . . ." My friend pulls up onto the next branch. ". . . You are having these dreams to learn a lesson."

"What am I supposed to be learning?" I ask.

"You tell me. What exactly did you pray for?"

"I have no idea."

"Yes, you do."

I sigh. "I asked God to prove He exists."

"Is that really it?" My friend knows there is something more to that prayer.

"Why does it matter?" I pull myself up onto the branch next to my friend so that we're eye level. "I don't even think I believe in God. Besides, why would He hear my one little prayer?"

"If you don't believe, then why did you pray?"

I pause. I did not expect that question. "I, um, asked for an experience I would never forget. I wanted God to prove He is real."

"Have you read any more of Genesis?"

"What does that have to do with it?"

"Your dreams," my friend emphasizes, almost seemingly annoyed. "They are the events from Genesis. You need to read more so you know what happens next."

"I asked God for an experience." I really exaggerate the word experience. "Why should I have to read something that's so old?"

"Because," my friend says, rolling their eyes, "the Bible is an experience."

I climb further up the tree. The ground is farther away from me now. From this height off the ground, I can nearly see the tops of the other trees around me. I smile. It feels good up here.

Boys, continue reading on the next page.
Girls, continue reading on page 77.

Boys, begin reading here.

…

My eyes open. Sunlight peeks through the cracks in the wooden beams above me.

Is this the same place?

The skin of an animal hangs in front of the doorway. I pull it aside and see the field that surrounded me in my last dream. This time, though, the plants are large and luscious.

I sigh. It will take a lot of work to harvest the field.

Eve is sitting with the two boys, who are older now. They must be older than I am in my real life. Their feet dangle in the water of a stream that runs beside the hut.

"Good morning," I say.

Eve glances over her shoulder, smiles, and waves me over to join them. "Praise God with us before we begin work today."

I sit with them. As the water runs against my toes, I feel a wave of peace wash over me. God is good.

"Praise God, who gives us food to eat, a place to live, and the love of family," Eve prays aloud. We all sit quietly for a few minutes, and I can almost hear God's voice calling my name, just as He did in Eden.

"Cain," Eve says to the older boy, "What are your plans today?"

"I'm going to begin the harvest."

"And Abel," Eve says as she turns to the other boy. "What are your plans?"

"We are expecting babies from our flock today."

"That's wonderful. Let me know if you need help." Eve stands up. "Let's get our day started."

Eve and I watch the boys walk away to begin the day's work. She hands me a basket and points to the apple trees. "Can you help with the fruit today? I think Abel is going to need my help with the ewes."

"I'd love to."

I walk to the beautiful orchard about a quarter of a mile from the hut. I pluck one apple and look up. The trees tower above me, heavy with fruit. I begin to climb.

Once I reach the middle branches, I stop and look out toward the fields. I watch as Cain harvests corn, pulling something that looks like a wooden wheelbarrow along behind him.

In the other direction, I see Abel rubbing the belly of a sheep. The sheep seems to be in pain. It must be time for the babies he mentioned.

Eve is near the hut. She hangs bundles of herbs, stopping every so often to tend to the fire.

My basket is full, so I climb down and carry it back to the hut. Eve helps herself to one of the apples and I do the same. With apples in hand, we begin to walk. So much has changed since my last dream.

Besides the hut, baskets, and wheelbarrow, I see several garden tools made of wood. There is a mound made of several stones piled on top of each other, like some kind of fire pit. Several animal skins, like the one on the hut, hang drying in the trees.

Though we have worked some of the land to live off of, most of it is still undisturbed. Only a few minutes into our walk, it feels as if we are surrounded by nothing but the trees, animals, and God's presence. This place is beautiful.

We walk around the path, eventually looping back and passing the hut. We go back to the stone, and see Cain and Abel waiting for us.

Abel holds a baby lamb and then sets him on the stone. "For my God, the firstborn of my flock. Thank You for the life You provide us."

As if He is standing among us, I hear God's voice. "Thank you," He says. "I am pleased with this gift."

Abel is thankful, and he kneels before God.

Cain dumps a basket of corn on the altar and smiles with pride. "For my God, from my harvest."

Unlike with Abel's gift, God is not pleased.

Cain's face changes. He looks angry, his eyes grow dark, and he turns away from us.

"Cain," Eve begins. "God wants your heart, not just your crops."

"God still loves you," I say as I set my hand on Cain's shoulder. He flinches. "Please don't let anger grow," I say.

Cain moves my hand away from his shoulder and walks away. Something about his attitude reminds me of myself and the way I've acted toward my parents.

Abel runs after him and calls out, "Brother! We will give an offering again. God may accept your next one."

The boys disappear into the tall stalks of corn. I hear a shout, then someone cries out in pain. Then, silence. Several minutes go by before Eve and I hear another sound. Cain stumbles out from between the corn stalks. I see blood on his hands and clothes.

"What happened?" Eve asks, as though she is afraid of the answer.

Cain does not make eye contact.

Eve's lip begins to quiver. I see a tear move down her cheek. "Please, tell me," she whispers.

Cain lifts his gaze to meet her eyes. "I was angry. I was jealous." He takes a deep breath then continues. "In my anger, I killed Abel, and now, God has banished me from His presence to wander for the rest of my life."

"Cain," Eve whispers in disbelief. "How can this be?"

Without a word, Cain turns from us and walks toward the wilderness.

Eve covers her face with her hands, falls to her knees, and lets out a heavy wail.

Unsure how to help her, I kneel down and hold her as I have seen Dad hold Mom when she was upset. As I let Eve cry, I begin to feel tears in my eyes as well.

Together, we begin to pray.

Continue reading on page 83.

Girls, begin reading here.

…

My eyes open. Sunlight peeks through the cracks in the wooden beams above me.

Is this the same place?

The skin of an animal hangs in front of the doorway. I pull it aside and see the field that surrounded me in my last dream. This time, though, the plants are large and luscious.

I sigh. It will take a lot of work to harvest the field.

Adam is sitting with the two boys, who are older now. They must be older than I am in my real life. Their feet dangle in the water of a stream that runs beside the hut.

"Good morning," I say.

Adam glances over his shoulder, smiles, and waves me over to join them. "Praise God with us before we begin work today."

I sit with them. As the water runs against my toes, I feel a wave of peace wash over me. God is good.

"Praise God, who gives us food to eat, a place to live, and the love of family," Adam prays aloud. We all sit quietly for a few minutes, and I can almost hear God's voice calling my name, just as He did in Eden.

"Cain," Adam says to the older boy, "What are your plans today?"

"I'm going to begin the harvest."

"And Abel," Adam says as he turns to the other boy. "What are your plans?"

"We are expecting babies from our flock today."

"That's wonderful. Let me know if you need help." Adam stands up. "Let's get our day started."

Adam and I watch the boys walk away to begin the day's work. He hands me a basket and points to the apple trees. "Can you help with the fruit today? I think Abel is going to need my help with the ewes."

"I'd love to."

I walk to the beautiful orchard about a quarter of a mile from the hut. I pluck one apple and look up. The trees tower above me, heavy with fruit. I begin to climb.

Once I reach the middle branches, I stop and look out toward the fields. I watch as Cain harvests corn, pulling something that looks like a wooden wheelbarrow along behind him.

In the other direction, I see Abel rubbing the belly of a sheep. The sheep seems to be in pain. It must be time for the babies he mentioned.

Adam is near the hut. He hangs bundles of herbs, stopping every so often to tend to the fire.

My basket is full, so I climb down and carry it back to the hut. Adam helps himself to one of the apples and I do the same. With apples in hand, we begin to walk. So much has changed since my last dream.

Besides the hut, baskets, and wheelbarrow, I see several garden tools made of wood. There is a mound made of several stones piled on top of each other, like some kind of fire pit. Several animal skins, like the one on the hut, hang drying in the trees.

Though we have worked some of the land to live off of, most of it is still undisturbed. Only a few minutes into our walk, it feels as if we are surrounded by nothing but the trees, animals, and God's presence. This place is beautiful.

We walk around the path, eventually looping back and passing the hut. We go back to the stone, and see Cain and Abel waiting for us.

Abel holds a baby lamb and then sets him on the stone. "For my God, the firstborn of my flock. Thank You for the life You provide us."

As if He is standing among us, I hear God's voice. "Thank you," He says. "I am pleased with this gift."

Abel is thankful, and he kneels before God.

Cain dumps a basket of corn on the altar and smiles with pride. "For my God, from my harvest."

Unlike with Abel's gift, God is not pleased.

Cain's face changes. He looks angry, his eyes grow dark, and he turns away from us.

"Cain," Adam begins. "God wants your heart, not just your crops."

"God still loves you," I say as I set my hand on Cain's shoulder. He flinches. "Please don't let anger grow," I say.

Cain moves my hand away from his shoulder and walks away. Something about his attitude reminds me of myself and the way I've acted toward my parents.

Abel runs after him and calls out, "Brother! We will give an offering again. God may accept your next one."

The boys disappear into the tall stalks of corn. I hear a shout, then someone cries out in pain. Then, silence. Several minutes go by before Adam and I hear another sound. Cain stumbles out from between the corn stalks. I see blood on his hands and clothes.

"What happened?" Adam asks, as though he is afraid of the answer.

Cain does not make eye contact.

Adam's lip begins to quiver. I see a tear move down his cheek. "Please, tell me," he whispers.

Cain lifts his gaze to meet Adam's eyes. "I was angry. I was jealous." He takes a deep breath then continues. "In my anger, I killed Abel, and now, God has banished me from His presence to wander for the rest of my life."

"Cain," I whisper in disbelief. "How can this be?"

Without a word, Cain turns from us and walks toward the wilderness.

I cover my face with my hands, fall to my knees, and let out a heavy wail.

Adam kneels next to me and wraps his arms around my shoulders, like Dad holds Mom when she is upset. As I cry, I hear Adam breathing heavily, and I realize he is crying with me.

Together, we pray.

Continue reading on page 83.

Chapter Six

power in prayer

I wake up at home. This time, I can't hide my tears.

My friend, already awake, looks at me. "Are you okay?"

"Yeah," I say, wiping tears from my eyes. "I feel like I was asleep for a week."

"You seem sad. Did you have another dream?"

I look toward my friend as a single tear runs from the corner of my eye and down my cheek. I take a deep breath and whisper, "Why did Cain kill Abel?"

"I'm not an expert," my friend starts, "but I think Cain got jealous because God liked Abel's offering better. Abel gave the firstborn of his flock, but Cain just gave some of his crops. There wasn't a real sacrifice in what he brought. Cain became so mad he ended up killing his brother."

We sit in silence for a moment.

"Was that your dream?" My friend asks.

I nod.

I go downstairs to see Mom kneeling beside her prayer chair, sticky notes in hand. Without thinking about what my friend might say and without worry of making Mom mad by interrupting her, I walk up to her and ask if I can sit with her for a few minutes while she prays.

Mom smiles.

I sit on the floor beside her, and Mom holds my hand after setting her sticky notes aside.

"Thank you, Lord," she says before continuing to mumble to herself.

I close my eyes for a moment.

When I open my eyes again, my friend is sitting in the chair across the room and appears to be praying.

Mom smiles and pats my knee, letting me know I don't have to stay. My friend continues to pray though, so I decide to give it a try too.

I clasp my hands together and close my eyes. I pray silently in my mind. Dear God, thank You for giving me a friend who understands me. Thank You for my mom and dad, and thank You for giving me an experience I will never forget.

After we pray, we eat breakfast together. I share the details of the dreams I have had with everyone. Mom says I should read Genesis. My friend gives me a knowing look. I smile and make a silent promise to myself I will finish reading Genesis and maybe even continue to the next book in the Bible too.

This moment, talking about the events from my dreams with the people I love, is more comforting than any other time I can remember. Perhaps it is because of my friend's strong faith, or maybe my Mom's constant prayer.

I can't deny my faith has grown in the past few months. Before, I wasn't sure God existed. Now, even though I am not sure what to believe about my dreams, or how they line up with the Bible, I do believe there's something powerful about prayer. More than anything else, I know prayer works. God is listening, and ready to give me an experience that will grow my faith.

discussion questions

---

1. What do you think it would feel like to live in the Garden of Eden? How might it be different from the world we live in today?

2. Why might someone feel embarrassed to talk about church with their friends? What would make it easier to share what you believe?

3. Have you ever had a friend who encourages you to be closer to God or to make good choices?

4. What are some ways you've helped a friend get closer to God? Have you ever shared something about your faith with them?

5. Have you ever seen God answer a prayer—big or small? How did it make you feel?

Author Bio

Ashley-Lynn Hall

Ashley has loved creating stories since she was a little girl. She started imagining stories at age seven and finally began putting them on paper in 2016. Since then, she has written many of her stories, but this book is her first based on the Bible, and it's especially close to her heart.

Ashley lives with her two amazing children. She enjoys reading, coloring, puzzles, organizing things, and playing board games and dominoes. She also loves quiet mornings outside and spending time with her church family.

While her kids are outgoing, Ashley is more of an observer—someone who watches the world closely and writes about what she sees and feels.

Her faith journey began when she was a child. After being teased for her love of books, she lost many friends, but one kind friend invited her to church. That's where

Ashley gave her life to Jesus. Years later, during a difficult season of feeling alone and deeply sad, she remembered the love she had felt at church as a child. She prayed for that love again, and God led her to a new church where she felt welcomed and at home from the very first visit. Through the love and grace of God—and the kindness of her church family—Ashley found healing, purpose, and a renewed passion for life.

Today, she writes to share that same message of hope, love, and faith with readers of all ages. She hopes her stories help others see that God is real, He speaks to us, and He loves us deeply.

Visit her website www.yelhsabooks.com to connect with Ashley. Her website features her name "Ashley" spelled backward to make "Yelsha," her creative way of distinguishing herself from other Ashleys.

OWL
OUR WRITTEN LIVES
Book Publishing & Writing Services
www.ourwrittenlives.com

www.ingramcontent.com/pod-product-compliance
Lightning Source LLC
Chambersburg PA
CBHW060748210726

48292CB00015B/2869